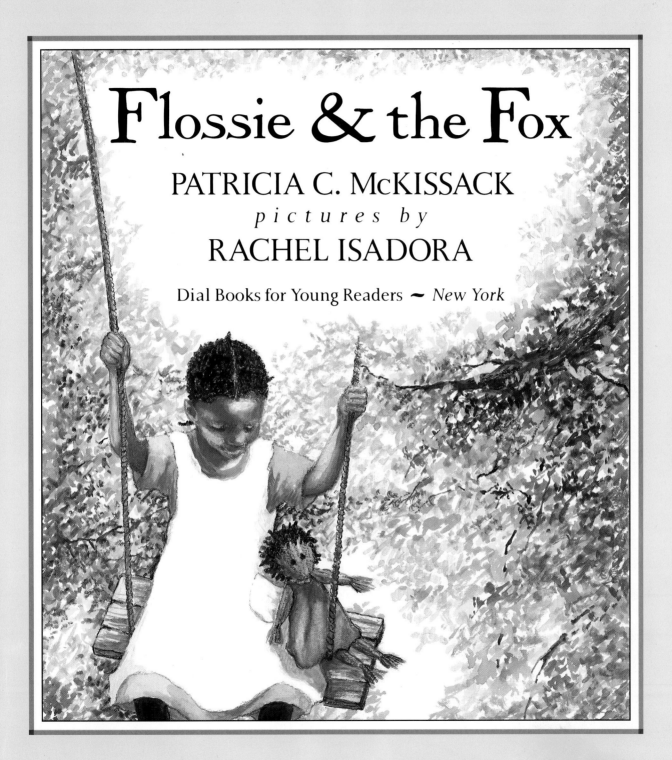

Flossie & the Fox

PATRICIA C. McKISSACK

pictures by

RACHEL ISADORA

Dial Books for Young Readers ~ *New York*

To my grandfather ~ For my Uncle Charlie
P.C.M.   R.I.

Published by Dial Books for Young Readers
375 Hudson Street / New York, New York 10014
Text copyright © 1986 by Patricia C. McKissack
Pictures copyright © 1986 by Rachel Isadora
All rights reserved
Printed in Hong Kong by South China Printing Co.
Design by Sara Reynolds
W
16 18 20 19 17

Library of Congress Cataloging-in-Publication Data
McKissack, Pat. 1944– Flossie & the fox.
Summary: A wily fox notorious for stealing eggs meets his match
when he encounters a bold little girl in the woods who insists
upon proof that he is a fox before she will be frightened.
[1. Foxes—Fiction.] I. Isadora, Rachel, ill.
II. Title. III. Title: Flossie and the fox.
PZ7.M478693F1   1986   [E]   86-2024
ISBN 0-8037-0250-7
ISBN 0-8037-0251-5 (lib. bdg.)

*The full-color artwork was prepared using pencil,
black ink, and watercolor. It was then
camera-separated and reproduced as red, blue,
yellow, and black halftones.*

AUTHOR'S NOTE

Long before I became a writer, I was a listener. On hot summer evenings our family sat on the porch and listened to my grandmother tell a hair-raising ghost story or watched my mother dramatize a Dunbar poem. But it was always a special treat when my grandfather took the stage. He was a master storyteller who charmed his audience with humorous stories told in the rich and colorful dialect of the rural South. I never wanted to forget them. So, it is through me that my family's storytelling legacy lives on.

Here is a story from my youth, retold in the same rich and colorful language that was my grandfather's. He began all his yarns with a question. "Did I ever tell you 'bout the time lil' Flossie Finley come out the Piney Woods heeling a fox?" I'd snuggle up beside him in the big porch swing, then he'd begin his tale. . . .

F LO-O-O-OSSIE!"

The sound of Big Mama's voice floated past the cabins in Sophie's Quarters, round the smokehouse, beyond the chicken coop, all the way down to Flossie Finley. Flossie tucked away her straw doll in a hollow log, then hurried to answer her grandmother's call.

"Here I am, Big Mama," Flossie said after catching her breath. It was hot, hotter than a usual Tennessee August day.

Big Mama stopped sortin' peaches and wiped her hands and face with her apron. "Take these to Miz Viola over at the Mc-Cutchin Place," she say reaching behind her and handing Flossie a basket of fresh eggs. "Seem like they been troubled by a fox. Miz Viola's chickens be so scared, they can't even now lay a stone." Big Mama clicked her teeth and shook her head.

"Why come Mr. J.W. can't catch the fox with his dogs?" Flossie asked, putting a peach in her apron pocket to eat later.

"Ever-time they corner that ol' slickster, he gets away. I tell you, that fox is one sly critter."

"How do a fox look?" Flossie asked. "I disremember ever seeing one."

Big Mama had to think a bit. "Chile, a fox be just a fox. But one thing for sure, that rascal loves eggs. He'll do most anything to get at some eggs."

Flossie tucked the basket under her arm and started on her

way. "Don't tarry now," Big Mama called. "And be particular 'bout them eggs."

"Yes'um," Flossie answered.

The way through the woods was shorter and cooler than the road route under the open sun. *What if I come upon a fox?* thought Flossie. *Oh well, a fox be just a fox. That aine so scary.*

Flossie commenced to skip along, when she come upon a critter she couldn't recollect ever seeing. He was sittin' 'side the road like he was expectin' somebody. Flossie skipped right up to him and nodded a greeting the way she'd been taught to do.

"Top of the morning to you, Little Missy," the critter replied. "And what is your name?"

"I be Flossie Finley," she answered with a proper curtsy. "I reckon I don't know who you be either."

Slowly the animal circled round Flossie. "I am a fox," he announced, all the time eyeing the basket of eggs. He stopped in front of Flossie, smiled as best a fox can, and bowed. "At your service."

Flossie rocked back on her heels then up on her toes, back and forward, back and forward . . . carefully studying the creature who was claiming to be a fox.

"Nope," she said at last. "I just purely don't believe it."

"You don't believe what?" Fox asked, looking way from the basket of eggs for the first time.

"I don't believe you a fox, that's what."

Fox's eyes flashed anger. Then he chuckled softly. "My dear child," he said, sounding right disgusted, "of course I'm a fox. A little girl like you should be simply terrified of me. Whatever do they teach children these days?"

Flossie tossed her head in the air. "Well, whatever you are, you sho' think a heap of yo'self," she said and skipped away.

Fox looked shocked. "Wait," he called. "You mean . . . you're not frightened? Not just a bit?"

Flossie stopped. Then she turned and say, "I aine never seen a fox before. So, why should I be scared of you and I don't even-now know you a real fox for a fact?"

Fox pulled himself tall. He cleared his throat. "Are you saying I must offer proof that I am a fox before you will be frightened of me?"

"That's just what I'm saying."

Lil' Flossie skipped on through the piney woods while that Fox fella rushed away lookin' for whatever he needed to prove he was really who he said he was.

Meanwhile Flossie stopped to rest 'side a tree. Suddenly Fox was beside her. "I have the proof," he said. "See, I have thick, luxurious fur. Feel for yourself."

Fox leaned over for Flossie to rub his back.

"Ummm. Feels like rabbit fur to me," she say to Fox. "Shucks! You aine no fox. You a rabbit, all the time trying to fool me."

"Me! A rabbit!" he shouted. "I have you know my reputation precedes me. I am the third generation of foxes who have out-smarted and out-run Mr. J.W. McCutchin's fine hunting dogs. I have raided some of the best henhouses from Franklin to Madison. Rabbit indeed! I am a fox, and you will act accordingly."

Flossie hopped to her feet. She put her free hand on her hip and patted her foot. "Unless you can show you a fox, I'll not accord you nothing!" And without further ceremony she skipped away.

Down the road a piece, Flossie stopped by a bubbly spring. She knelt to get a drink of water. Fox came up to her and said, "I have a long pointed nose. Now that should be proof enough."

"Don't prove a thing to me." Flossie picked some wild flowers. "Come to think of it," she said matter-of-fact-like, "rats got long pointed noses." She snapped her fingers. "That's it! You a rat trying to pass yo'self off as a fox."

That near 'bout took Fox's breath away. "I beg your pardon," he gasped.

"You can beg all you wanna," Flossie say skipping on down the road. "That still don't make you no fox."

"I'll teach you a thing or two, young lady," Fox called after her. "You just wait and see."

Before long Flossie came to a clearing. A large orange tabby was sunning on a tree stump. "Hi, pretty kitty," the girl say and rubbed the cat behind her ears. Meanwhile Fox slipped from behind a clump of bushes.

"Since you won't believe me when I tell you I am a fox," he said stiffly, "perhaps you will believe that fine feline creature, toward whom you seem to have some measure of respect."

Flossie looked at the cat and winked her eye. "He sho' use a heap o' words," she whispered.

Fox beckoned for Cat to speak up. Cat jumped to a nearby log and yawned and stretched—then she answered. "This is a fox because he has sharp claws and yellow eyes," she purred.

Fox seemed satisfied. But Flossie looked at Cat. She looked at Fox, then once more at both just to be sure. She say, "All due respect, Miz Cat, but both y'all got sharp claws and yellow eyes. So…that don't prove nothing, 'cep'n both y'all be cats."

Fox went to howling and running round in circles. He was plum beside himself. "I am a fox and I know it," he shouted. "This is absurd!"

"No call for you to use that kind of language," Flossie said and she skipped away.

"Wait, wait," Fox followed pleading. "I just remembered some-thing. It may be the solution to this—this horrible situation."

"Good. It's about time."

"I-I-I have a bushy tail." Fox seemed to perk up. "That's right," he said. "All foxes are known for their fluffy, bushy tails. That has got to be adequate proof."

"Aine got to be. You got a bushy tail. So do squirrels." Flossie pointed to one overhead leaping from branch to branch in the tree tops. "Here, have a bite of peach," she said, offering Fox first bite of her treat.

But Fox was crying like a natural born baby. "No, no, no," he sobbed. "If I promise you I'm a fox, won't that do?"

Flossie shook her head no.

"Oh, woe is me," Fox hollered. "I may never recover my confidence."

Flossie didn't stop walking. "That's just what I been saying. You just an ol' confidencer. Come tellin' me you was a fox, then can't prove it. Shame on you!"

Long about that time, Flossie and the fox came out of the

woods. Flossie cupped her hands over her eyes and caught sight
of McCutchin Quarters and Miz Viola's cabin. Fox didn't notice
a thing; he just followed behind Flossie begging to be believed.

"Give me one last chance," he pleaded.

Flossie turned on her heels. "Okay. But just this once more."

Fox tried not to whimper, but his voice was real unsteady-like. "I-I have sharp teeth and I can run exceedingly fast." He waited for Flossie to say something.

Slowly the girl rocked from heel to toe . . . back and forward. "You know," she finally said, smiling, "it don't make much difference what I think anymore."

"What?" Fox asked. "Why?"

"Cause there's one of Mr. J.W. McCutchin's hounds behind you. He's got sharp teeth and can run fast too. And, by the way that hound's lookin', it's all over for you!"

With a quick glance back Fox dashed toward the woods. "The hound knows who I am!" he shouted. "But I'm not worried. I sure

can out-smart and out-run one of Mr. J. W. McCutchin's miserable mutts any old time of the day, because like I told you, I am a fox!"

"I know," said Flossie. "I know." And she turned toward Miz Viola's with the basket of eggs safely tucked under her arm.